A Nuer Tale

What's So Funny, Ketu?

retold by VERNA AARDEMA

pictures by MARC BROWN

A Puffin Pied Piper

What's So Funny, Ketu?: A Nuer Tale is adapted from
Otwe, by Verna Aardema, published by Coward-McCann, Inc.,
1960. The tale is a retelling of "The Man and the Snake"
in *Nuer Customs and Folklore,* by Ray Huffman, published
by Oxford University Press, London, 1931, with rights
by the International African Institute, London.

Published by Dial Books for Young Readers
A Division of Penguins Books USA Inc.
375 Hudson Street
New York, New York 10014
Text copyright © 1982 by Verna Aardema
Pictures copyright © 1982 by Marc Brown
All rights reserved
Library of Congress Catalog Card Number: 82-70195
Printed in Hong Kong
First Pied Piper Printing 1989
(b)
10 9 8 7 6 5 4 3 2

A Pied Piper Book is a registered trademark of
Dial Books for Young Readers,
a division of Penguin Books USA Inc.,
® TM 1,163,686 and ® TM 1,054,312.

WHAT'S SO FUNNY, KETU?
is published in a hardcover edition by
Dial Books for Young Readers.
ISBN 0-14-054722-3

*The art for each picture consists of a
pencil and ink drawing with three overlays
prepared in gouache and ink and reproduced
in black, brown, yellow, and red halftone.*

For my young friend George McClane
V.A.

For Verna Aardema, storyteller extraordinaire
M.B.

In Africa, near the Mountains of the Moon, there once lived a man named Ketu. He was a happy man. A big laugh lived inside him. But it was *that* that got him into trouble.

It happened like this.

One day Ketu heard his dog yelping, *kao, kao, kao,* behind the hut. He investigated and found the dog worrying a harmless little snake.

Ketu scolded the dog and sent him slinking off, *prada, prada, prada,* with his tail between his legs.

The little snake raised its head and said, "Thank you, Man. You are kind. I'm going to give you a gift."

Ketu laughed, *tu-e, tu-e, tu-e!* "What can a small creature like yourself give to me?" he asked.

"A magic gift," said the snake. "From now on, you will hear animals think. But you must not tell anyone, or you will die!"

Ketu was not sure he wanted such a gift. He tried to protest. But the little snake had vanished!

That night Ketu's wife, Nyaloti, put their baby into her basket bed. She tucked a pacifier, made from the neck of a tiny gourd, into the baby's mouth. And she patted her to sleep, *pah, pah, pah!*

Then Ketu fastened the door. And he and Nyaloti lay down on their low beds along the walls of the hut.

Soon they heard a mosquito going *zeee* around the door. And Ketu heard it say to itself, "I know they're in there! Fat, juicy people! But I can't find a big-enough crack!"

Ketu laughed, *ge-e, ge-e, ge-e.* He laughed so hard, he rolled off his bed—GU–MAPP!

Nyaloti cried, "What's so funny, Ketu?"

"Nothing!" said Ketu as he climbed back into bed. He could not tell her.

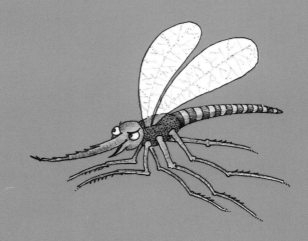

Soon a rat tried the door. It could not get in either. But it found a hole under the roof and came in there.

Ta, ta, ta, went the little feet of the rat, back and forth across the floor. Then Ketu heard it say to itself, "I wonder where that so-so woman keeps her butter!"

Ketu exploded with laughter, *kye, kye, kye!* He laughed so hard, he scared the rat. And it leaped up onto Nyaloti's bed—TWUM—in the middle of Nyaloti!

"*A-a-a-a!*" she screamed. "Get that rat off me!"

The rat leaped to the wall and scurried out through the hole.

Nyaloti sat up in bed. She said, "Ketu, I think your big laugh made that rat jump on me! What were you laughing about?"

"Nothing!" said Ketu. "It was nothing."

"Nothing! *Tuh!*" sniffed Nyaloti. For by then the baby was crying, *ke-yaa, ke-yaa, ke-yaa.* And Nyaloti had to get her back to sleep.

The next morning Ketu fetched the cow from the shed and tied her to a tree so that Nyaloti could milk her. Soon he saw his wife coming with her big calabash bowl.

The cow saw her too. And Ketu heard her say to herself, "Here she comes to steal my milk! This time I just won't give any milk. And my calf will drink it afterward!"

Ketu laughed, *ge-e, ge-e, ge-e!* He laughed so hard, he scared the cow. And she galloped, *nun-tun, nun-tun,* around the tree.

Nyaloti set the bowl down so she could scold her husband with both hands. She said, "What's so funny, Ketu? Now you've frightened the cow with that silly laugh! Were you laughing at me?"

"No," said Ketu as he walked away. "It was nothing."

The cow did not give any milk. Nyaloti didn't get a drop in her bowl.

But the calf drank from her mother until her belly was round and fat. It was as if she knew the saying, Lest good food wastes, let the belly bust.

That evening at milking time the cow still would not give milk. Nyaloti called Ketu. "Look," she said, "no milk again. Our baby is ill for want of it. That calf is killing our daughter!"

The cow swung her big head around and looked at Nyaloti. And Ketu heard her say to herself, "What! *My* daughter is killing *her* daughter!"

Ketu tried to hold back the laughter. But it burst out between his fingers, *gug, gug, gug!*

The cow was so startled, she kicked and sent the bowl rolling, *denki, denki, denki,* in the dirt.

"Now see what you did!" cried Nyaloti. "You and that stupid laugh. I'm going to tell the chief."

Nyaloti told the chief.

The chief called Ketu and all his wise men to the Tree of Justice in the middle of the village. Nyaloti came too, with the baby in a basket on her head. And many other people came, just to hear the palaver.

"Ketu," said the chief, "your wife tells me you laugh when there is nothing to laugh about. Is that true?"

"Oh, Chief," said Ketu, "I never laugh without a reason. But I can't tell the reason. If I tell, I will die!"

"Nonsense!" exclaimed the chief. "Talking never killed anyone!"

Nyaloti said, "He laughs at me, Chief. I'm the only one around."

"No," said Ketu. "It isn't that!"

"If you don't laugh at your wife, what do you laugh about?" demanded the chief.

Someone shouted, "Tell us, Ketu. We want to laugh too!"

The chief said, "Ketu, if you will not tell, your wife will have to take the baby and go back to live with her father."

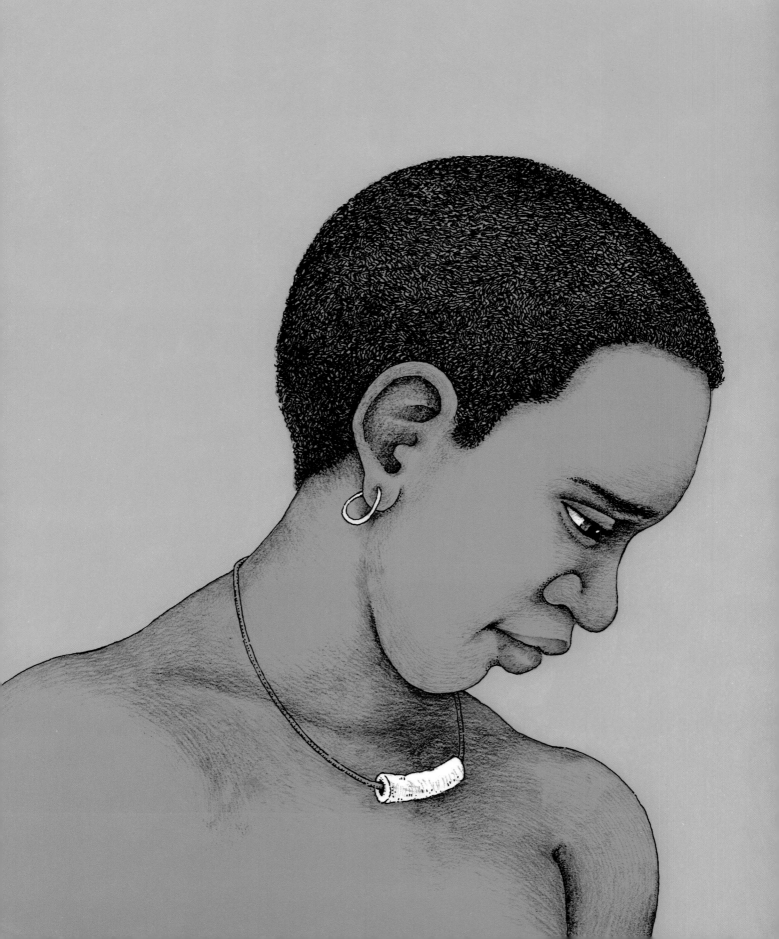

Ketu's head drooped. He dug his toe into the sand at his feet, *sa, sa, sa*. He didn't know what to do.

Just then his baby began to cry, *ke-yaa, ke-yaa, ke-yaa!* Ketu watched as Nyaloti lowered the basket and lifted out their beautiful baby. The pacifier he had made dangled from the baby's fat little wrist.

Suddenly Ketu knew that no matter what happened, he could not let his wife and baby go. So he told about the little snake, the magic gift, and the funny thoughts of the animals.

Then KWAM! He fell over dead!

"Look!" cried the oldest wise man. "We made him do what he should not have done. And he has had to pay with his life!"

Nyaloti and many of the women began to wail, *wolu, wolu, wolu!*

The chief shook his head sadly.

Presently the little snake appeared. It put its shiny head on Ketu's head.

Ketu opened his eyes. He turned his head in time to see the little snake wriggle off into the weeds. And he heard it say to itself, "Snoopy! That's what they are! They can't let a man keep a secret!"

Ketu laughed, *kye, kye, kye!* He rolled on the ground with laughter.

The oldest wise man bent over him and asked, "What's so funny, Ketu?"

The chief cried, "Don't ask him *that*!"

And Nyaloti said, "Laugh all you want, Ketu. I'll never make palaver about it again!"

Then all the people began to laugh. They laughed so hard, they scared the baby. And above the sounds of laughter was heard the crying of the baby, KE-YAA, KE-YAA, KE-YAA!